Donated By *Book Fair*
AGS P.T.O. *Profits 11/2003*

DATE DUE DISCARD

E   Edwardson, Debby Dahl
EDW   Whale snow
c.1
             $15.95

DEMCO

Whale
Snow

Debby Dahl Edwardson ● *Illustrated by Annie Patterson*

TALEWINDS

A Charlesbridge Imprint

For my sons Amiqqaq and Ahmaogak; and for my daughters Ayałhuq, Qiḷaavsuk, Aaluk, Manuluuraq, and Ahgeak. May you always remember whale happiness—D. E.

To Gramma Vivi—A. P.

Published by Charlesbridge
85 Main Street, Watertown, MA 02472
(617) 926-0329
www.charlesbridge.com

Library of Congress Cataloging-in-Publication Data

Edwardson, Debby Dahl.
  Whale snow / Debby Dahl Edwardson ; illustrated by Annie Patterson.
    p. cm.
Summary: At the first whaling feast of the season, a young Iñupiaq boy learns about the importance of the bowhead whale to his people and their culture. Includes facts about Iñupiats and the bowhead whale.
  ISBN 1-57091-393-5 (reinforced for library use)
  1. Iñupiat—Juvenile fiction. [1. Iñuit—Fiction. 2. Eskimos—Fiction. 3. Bowhead whale—Fiction. 4. Whales—Fiction. 5. Whaling—Fiction.] I. Patterson, Annie, ill. II. Title.
  PZ7.E2657 Wh 2003
  [E]—dc21   2002010536

Printed in Singapore
(hc) 10 9 8 7 6 5 4 3 2 1

Illustrations painted in watercolor on Arches paper
Display type set in Papyrus and text type set in Sabon
Designed by Susan Mallory Sherman
Color separations, printing, and binding by Imago
Production supervision by Linda Jackson

The Iñupiaq Language

Iñupiaq hasn't always been a written language. Through the long winter nights of the Arctic, young people learned by listening to the stories of the elders, told in Iñupiaq. These stories taught history and culture and were passed from generation to generation through the memory of the people. In the 1800s when commercial whalers crowded the North, the Iñupiat were forced to learn and speak English. At schools, Iñupiat children were punished for speaking Iñupiaq. During this time the Iñupiaq language and culture were threatened, but the Iñupiat fought to preserve their cultures by recording their stories and putting their language into writing. Today schools and cultural centers teach Iñupiaq history, language, and culture.

To read *Whale Snow* in Iñupiaq and for more information on the Iñupiaq language, check out our Web site at www.charlesbridge.com.

Words to Know

aaka (AH-ka): grandmother

aapa (AH-pa): grandfather

aarigaa (AH-dee-gah): Wow! Wonderful!

aġvaktuni quviasuun (aga-VAHK-too-nee coo-VEE-ah-soon): whale happiness

aġviq (AGA-vik): bowhead whale

amii? (AH-mee): right?

Amiqqaq (AH-mik-kahk): the boy's name

apuyyaq (AH-pooh-yahk): snow house

apun (AH-poon): snow

ii (ee): yes

iḷitqusia aġviġum (ill-LIT-coo-see AGA-vee-oom): spirit-of-the-whale

Iñupiaq (in-YU-pea-ahk): Adjective form of "Iñupiat," and the name of the language. It can be used as a noun to refer to a single person.

Iñupiat (in-YU-pea-at): The name used by Eskimos living in the northernmost portion of Alaska. Literally this means "real people" of the Arctic.

tupiq (TOO-pick): a white, canvas tent

uunaalik (oon-AH-lik): cooked whale meat and blubber

uqsruagnaq (ook-rue-AGA-nuck): whale snow

The snow fell in big flakes, fat as eiderdown. The snow fell soft and slow like shreds of cotton grass floating down from the sky. Amiqqaq leaned up against the window, wishing he were out on the ocean ice, out in the big tent with his papa, out with the whalers.

Amiqqaq's grandma stood by the hot stove frying Eskimo donuts. The hot donuts made the window steamy, made the house smell sweet. Amiqqaq pressed his nose against the window. The cold glass felt good. Outside, snowflakes as big as birds whirled and swirled in the wind.

"Look, Aaka," Amiqqaq called. "Fat snow!"

"Hmmm," said his aaka, stretching out handfuls of sweet dough. "Whale snow."

"Whale snow?"

Aaka nodded her head.

"Ii, whale snow. Whale snow comes when a whale has given itself to the People."

"Which people?" Amiqqaq asked. "Which people has the whale given itself to, Aaka?"

"Ah," said Aaka, her eyes happy, "you'll see. Soon, you will see."

Amiqqaq heard the roar of Papa's skidoo. Papa raced into the house brushing fat snowflakes from his parka.

"I have brought the Amiqqaq whaling flag," Papa said.

Aaka smiled, nodding her head. "Aarigaa!" she said.

"Are we going to hang the flag?" asked Amiqqaq.

"Ii," said Papa. "Of course. We'll hang the flag to let everyone know it's time to celebrate. But first, I must go back out to help the whalers prepare the whale. A whaling captain can't be lazy." He tousled Amiqqaq's hair.

Amiqqaq stood up as tall as he could.

"Can I go, Papa, please? Can I go help? I'm not lazy!"

Papa looked at Aaka. Aaka looked at Amiqqaq and smiled.

"The last time the Amiqqaq crew was given a whale was the day you were born. That's why we named you Amiqqaq," Aaka said.

Papa chuckled.

"Hurry up, Amiqqaq," he said. "Get dressed. Let's go see the Amiqqaq whale."

Outside the wind blew hard, pushing against Amiqqaq's back like a heavy hand.

"Strong wind, Papa," Amiqqaq said.

"Ii, it's a whale wind," said Papa. "Every whale has its own weather. The Amiqqaq whale came to us in windy weather. This is a whale wind."

"But where is the Amiqqaq whale?"

"Ah," said Papa. "You'll see."

Papa's skidoo raced out onto the frozen ocean,
out into the strong wind, out past massive chunks
of blue-green ice, bigger than skidoos, huge as houses.

Soon, they saw the Amiqqaq whale. It lay on the snow-covered ice like an enormous black mountain. Beside it, Papa's big white tent flapped in the wind, looking as small as a playhouse. Many, many people crowded around the Amiqqaq whale, smiling and hugging and crying tears of joy.

Amiqqaq's momma came out from the billowing white tent holding steaming mugs of hot coffee.

Amiqqaq's papa lifted him up to the very top of the enormous whale. Everyone cheered.

"Aarigaa! Amiqqaq's whale!"

Amiqqaq's momma lifted him down.

"Momma, I feel happy inside. Inside is like a giant smile. Bigger than a house. Wider than a whole village."

"Ii," said Momma. "You feel whale happiness. When the spirit-of-the-whale gives itself to the People, it brings great happiness. This is whale happiness."

Amiqqaq looked up at the great big whale. "I can see the spirit-of-the-whale, Momma!"

"No, Amiqqaq," his momma said gently. "That is not the spirit-of-the-whale. That is only the parka the spirit-of-the-whale wears."

"But where is the spirit-of-the-whale, Momma?"

"Ah," said his momma, hugging him, "You'll see. You'll see soon."

Soon his uncles were carrying big boxes of food in and out of Amiqqaq's house. Amiqqaq's momma and aaka made uunaalik, cooking fat chunks of whale meat and maktak in big pots of boiling water. The house was steamy with smells that made his mouth water.

Everyone in the whole village came to eat at Amiqqaq's house. People filed in and out of the door all day long.

His aunties ladled spoons of sweet cooked fruit into many, many cups. They dished out big plates full of steaming uunaalik. They gave people Eskimo donuts and cooked fruit and plates piled high with uunaalik.

Amiqqaq sat on the floor by his aapa. Aapa cut small chunks of uunaalik for Amiqqaq to eat. Uunaalik made his belly warm. The warmth tingled in his toes, making him smile. Everybody smiled and laughed. Amiqqaq's house was packed with happiness.

"Aapa," Amiqqaq whispered, "I know where the spirit-of-the-whale is." Amiqqaq's aapa leaned down close to Amiqqaq.

"Tell me, Amiqqaq, where is the spirit-of-the-whale?"

"The spirit-of-the-whale is in the fat snow and strong wind, Aapa," Amiqqaq said. "The spirit-of-the-whale is right here in my house, making people smile and laugh. Together."

"Ii, Amiqqaq," Aapa said, nodding his head. "Ii."

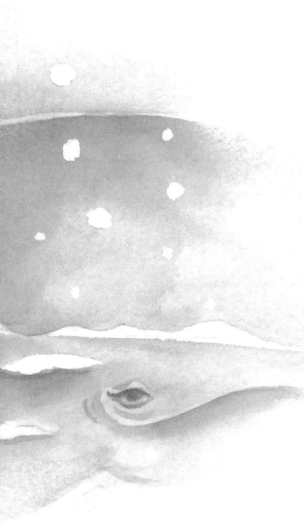

"But where does the spirit-of-the-whale go after, Aapa?"

"After?"

"After the people leave."

"Ah," said Aapa with a wink, "the spirit-of-the-whale goes back to the sea, as you will someday see. It goes back to the sea."

"But we will still have whale happiness, Aapa, amii?"

"Yes, Amiqqaq. We will still have happiness. Whale happiness is the gift the whale leaves."

The Bowhead and the Iñupiat: A Partnership

When springtime comes to the Arctic coast of Alaska and the ocean ice splits open, bowhead whales swim northward. Iñupiat whalers set their white tents on the edge of the ice waiting, as they have done for centuries, for the return of the whales.

The Iñupiat have long shared a special bond with the bowheads. Legend tells of an Iñupiaq shaman who visited the whales and learned a message of sharing and cooperation. The Iñupiat believe that whales choose to give themselves to worthy whaling crews that have emulated the spirit-of-the-whale by avoiding conflict and practicing generosity. This spirituality, passed down through generations, is the same tradition followed in *Whale Snow.*

But the bond between the Iñupiat and the whale is more than spiritual. Less than 100 years ago, the whale provided the Iñupiat with homes, heat, food, and light. Living on the treeless tundra, the Iñupiat used the huge whalebones, along with driftwood, as the framework for their sod homes. Whale oil provided heat and light, while meat and blubber provided a major source of food. Even bowhead baleen found use in the creation of baskets, nets, cups, and sled runners.

This relationship was threatened in 1977 when the International Whaling Commission (IWC) called for a ban on Iñupiat whaling. Formed by the commercial whaling nations of the world, IWC did not understand the special relationship the Iñupiat have always shared with the whale. Bowheads have given the Iñupiat physical and spiritual sustenance.

In response to the IWC ban, Iñupiat whaling captains formed the Alaskan Eskimo Whaling Commission (AEWC), which today regulates Iñupiat whaling by agreement with the federal government. Through AEWC, the Iñupiat have sponsored scientific studies of bowheads. Using underwater microphones, called hydrophones, scientists can follow whale movements and listen to individual whale voices.

Today the Iñupiat live in modern homes, but hold fast to the special culture surrounding the whale. Preparation for whaling is a year-round process and as in the old days, when magical amulets and songs were used to call the whales, spirituality is still an important part of the hunt.